Book 2

Ick and Crud

Mystery in the Barn

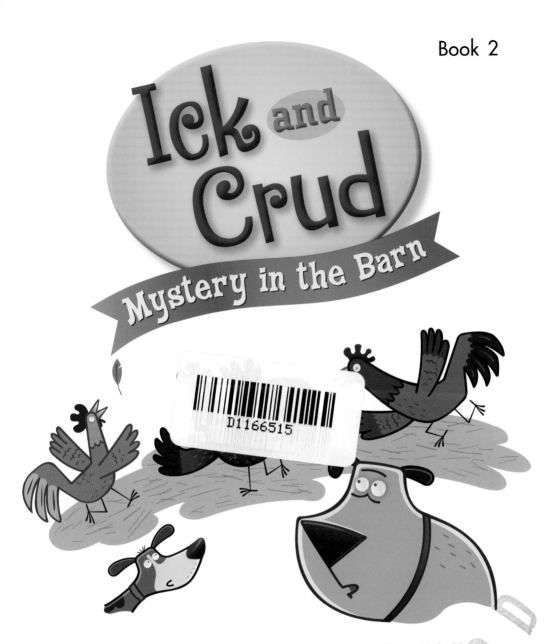

by Wiley Blevins • illustrated by Jim Paillot

RED CHAIR PRESS

Funny Bone Books

and Funny Bone Readers are produced and published by

Red Chair Press LLC   PO Box 333   South Egremont, MA 01258-0333

www.redchairpress.com

About the Author

Wiley Blevins has taught elementary school in both the United States and South America. He has also written over 60 books for children and 15 for teachers, as well as created reading programs for schools in the U.S. and Asia with Scholastic, Macmillan/McGraw-Hill, Houghton-Mifflin Harcourt, and other publishers. Wiley currently lives and writes in New York City.

About the Artist

Jim Paillot is a dad, husband and illustrator. He lives in Arizona with his family and two dogs and any other animal that wants to come in out of the hot sun. When not illustrating, Jim likes to hike, watch cartoons and collect robots.

Publisher's Cataloging-In-Publication Data

Names: Blevins, Wiley. | Paillot, Jim, illustrator.

Title: Ick and Crud. Book 2, Mystery in the barn / by Wiley Blevins ; illustrated by Jim Paillot.
Other Titles: Mystery in the barn

Description: South Egremont, MA : Red Chair Press, [2017] | Series: First chapters | Interest age level: 005-007. | Summary: "Something big is happening in the barn. The animals are all making a fuss. No good dog can resist the chance to sniff out the mystery."--Provided by publisher.

Identifiers: LCCN 2016947291 | ISBN 978-1-63440-186-9 (library hardcover) | ISBN 978-1-63440-189-0 (paperback) | ISBN 978-1-63440-192-0 (ebook)

Subjects: LCSH: Barns--Juvenile fiction. | Dogs--Juvenile fiction. | CYAC: Barns--Fiction. | Dogs--Fiction. | LCGFT: Detective and mystery fiction.

Classification: LCC PZ7.B618652 Icm 2017 (print) | LCC PZ7.B618652 (ebook) | DDC [E]--dc23

Printed in the United States of America
0517 1P CGBF17

Table of Contents

Meet the Characters

Crud

Ick

Miss Puffy

Bob

Something Big!

Ick and Crud set out to have another
fun day. They raced through their yard,
skipping and yapping until they came to
Mrs. Martin's fence.

"Stop," yelled Crud.

"Why?" asked Ick.

"The mud," said Crud.

"Oh, right," said Ick. "Good thinking."

Miss Puffy hopped on top of the fence.

She shook like she had just seen something
very scary.

"Should we ask?" asked Ick.

"No," said Crud. Miss Puffy shook again. "I give up," said Crud. "What's bugging you now?"

Miss Puffy purred. "I thought you'd never ask. Something BIG is about to happen."

Just then a noise rang out from the barn in the back of Mrs. Martin's yard.

"Did you just come from the barn?" asked Ick.

"Oh, I wouldn't be caught dead in the barn," said Miss Puffy. "No classy cat would."

"Then it sounds like our kind of place," said Crud. "Let's go, Ick. Something big is about to happen there!"

What Could Go Wrong?

Ick and Crud jumped over the fence. *Splat!*
"How soon we forget," moaned Crud.
He and Ick shook off the mud, then raced
down the hill and to the barn. They
skidded to a stop at the big, red door.

They leaned their ears against the door. A loud, low moo shook it. "What is that?" asked Ick. "A horse?"

"No," said Crud.

Then a squealing oink shook the door. "What is that?" asked Ick. "A chicken?"

"No," said Crud.

Finally, a chorus of squawks shook the door. "What is that?" asked Ick. "A bunch of elephants?"

"No," said Crud. "But something big *is* going on! Should we?" asked Crud.

"I will if you will," said Ick.

"Then let's go inside," said Crud.

Crud nudged open the barn door. A screech shot out.

Ick froze. "Do we *really* have to go inside?" he asked.

"What could go wrong in a barn?" asked Crud.

Ick gulped. He hid behind Crud as they tiptoed inside. Suddenly...

The cows stopped counting their spots. The pigs stopped curling their tails. And the chickens stopped polishing their eggs.

A mouse poked her head out from behind a barrel.

"It's just those two dogs from over the fence," she said. "All clear." So, the animals went back to mooing, oinking, squawking, and doing what animals do in a barn when no one is watching.

"What do we do now?" asked Ick.

"Let's see if someone knows the *big* thing that is about to happen."

So Ick and Crud shuffled over to the cows. "Moo," said one of the cows. "Poo to you, too," said Ick.

"Do you know what is about to happen?" asked Crud. The cow nodded and pointed to the pigpen.

So Ick and Crud skipped over to the
pigs. "Oink," said one of the pigs.

"Boink to you, too," said Ick.

"Do you know what is about to
happen?" asked Crud.

All the pigs began to squeal and run
around the pen. But not one answered
Crud.

"Okay," said Crud. "Let's ask the chickens."

"Yes," said Ick. "The chickens always know what's going on."

"Cluck, cluck, squawk," shouted the chickens.

"Click, clack, squeak to you, too," said Ick.

"Do you know what is about to happen?" asked Crud. "Yes," said one of the chickens. "But we are missing our rooster. We can't tell you until he comes back."

Cluck, Squawk, Help!

"What do we do now?" asked Ick.

"Let's explore the barn," said Crud. "That will pass the time."

Ick and Crud ran through the barn, stuck their heads in every stall, hopped over buckets, leaped over shovels, jumped over mice, then climbed up the ladder, and plopped onto the hay.

"That didn't take long," said Ick. "So, what do we do now?"

"I know," said Crud. "Let's play hide-n-seek."

"Yes," said Ick. "That's my favorite game. How do you play hide-n-seek again?"

"I will hide," said Crud. "Then you count to ten. When you're done, you look for me."

"Got it," said Ick. He covered his eyes as Crud snuck away to hide. "1... 2... 3... 8... 16... 97... 33... 81... 82... 10."

Ick opened his eyes. "Here I come," he yelled. Ick looked here. Ick looked there. He looked up. He looked down. And he looked all around. But he didn't find Crud. He plopped back onto the hay.

"This game is not fun without Crud," he moaned.

Then he felt something move in the hay.
"BOO!" yelled Crud, as he popped out.

"AAAAAGGGGHHHH!" screamed Ick.
"You scared the doggie bones out of me."
Then he jumped on Crud and rolled in
the hay. They rolled and rolled and rolled
until...

"Cluck, squawk, HELP!" rang out from
inside the barn.

"Who is that?" asked Ick.

"One of the chickens," said Crud. "Let's
go find out what's wrong."

Sit, Sit, Ouch!

Ick and Crud climbed down the ladder and raced to the chickens.

"It's about to happen! It's about to happen!" yelled all the chickens. And they ran around and around clucking and clacking and squeaking and squawking.

Crud grabbed one of them by the wings. He looked the chicken in its beady eyes. "*What* is about to happen?" he asked.

The chicken pointed to two nests filled with eggs. "The rooster is their daddy. He isn't back," the chicken said. "We must all go find him. Can you sit on the eggs until we get back?"

"We like to sit," said Ick.

"Yes," said Crud. "We'll do it."

The two sat on the nests. But before long… Ick felt a wiggle under his butt. "Oh, my," he said.

Crud felt a squiggle under his butt.
"This feels funny," he said.

Then each felt a poke. And another
poke. Poke. Poke. Poke. "Ouch!" yelled
Ick and Crud.

They hopped off the nests and looked down to see two nests filled with little yellow chicks.

"Peep," said one of the chicks.

"Jeep?" asked Ick.

"Peep, peep, peep," said the other chicks. Then one little chick hopped on the edge of the nest.

"Are you our daddy?" the chick asked.

"Daddy?" asked Ick.

"Oh, no," said Crud. "Run!"

And they raced out of the barn, up the
hill, over the fence, and into their yard.

"It's good to be home," said Ick.

"Yes," said Crud. "It's good to be in a place where nothing *big* is about to happen. Goodnight, buddy."

"Goodnight."